The Big Book of Careers

Planning Your Path Ahead

Vandana Verma

DIAMOND BOOKS

www.diamondbooks.in

Publisher : **Diamond Pocket Books (P) Ltd.**
X-30, Okhla Industrial Area, Phase-II
New Delhi-110020
Phone : 011-40712200
E-mail : wecare@diamondbooks.in
Website : www.diamondbooks.in
Edition : 2025
Printed By : Repro (India)

Preface

This book is designed to help students in Grades 9 to 12 understand themselves, explore career options, and make informed decisions about their academic and professional future. In today's fast-changing world, early career planning is not just helpful—it's essential. This guide aligns with India's NEP 2020 and NCF 2023 to empower students with skills, clarity, and confidence in navigating their career journeys.

- Vandana Verma

FOREWORD

By a School Career Counselor or Educator

"Career planning is no longer a one-time decision but a journey of self-discovery. As a counselor, I've seen how empowered students become when they are equipped with the right tools and guidance. This book blends personal reflection with practical tools, ensuring that students don't just dream big, but act on their goals strategically."

Table of Contents

Chapter 1

Know Yourself

The First Step to Career Planning

Meet Ayaan and Meera, two Grade 10 students. Ayaan loves tinkering with gadgets and dreams of inventing something big. Meera, on the other hand, has always loved storytelling and drama club. Both are passionate and curious—but when their school asked them to choose subjects for Grade 11, they felt confused.

"Should I go for Science even though I like writing?" Meera wondered.

"Is Engineering my only path?" Ayaan asked.

This is a common story. Students are often expected to make big decisions without truly understanding themselves first. That's why this chapter is all about one thing: You.

Because the foundation of good career planning isn't a list of job options—it's self-awareness.

Explore the Concept: What Does "Knowing Yourself" Mean?

When we talk about knowing yourself, we mean three key things:

1. Your Interests – What do you enjoy doing?
2. Your Strengths (Skills) – What are you good at?
3. Your Values & Personality – What kind of life matters to you?

Each of these shapes the kind of career that will make you feel successful—not just in earning money, but in being happy and fulfilled.

1. Your Interests

Interests are the activities, topics, and ideas that you naturally enjoy. They can be academic (like math or science) or non-academic (like gardening, music, or solving puzzles).

Ask Yourself:

- What subjects do I enjoy at school?
- What do I love doing in my free time?
- What topics do I often search about online or in books?

2. Your Strengths (Skills)

These are the things you do well. Strengths can be:

- Hard skills: Writing, coding, designing, solving math problems.
- Soft skills: Communication, teamwork, leadership, empathy.

Activity:

Tick the ones that feel like you:

Skill	Description
Communication	I explain things well to others.
Problem-solving	I enjoy solving challenges or fixing things.
Creativity	I think of new ideas often.
Organizing	I plan things and keep my work neat.
Math/Logical Thinking	I like numbers, patterns, or logic puzzles.
Empathy	I understand others' feelings easily.

3. Your Personality & Values

- Are you outgoing or quiet?
- Do you like working alone or with others?
- Do you care about making a difference? Stability? Recognition?

These preferences matter when choosing a career. A creative extrovert may enjoy marketing, while a quiet problem-solver may thrive in coding or data analysis.

In the Real World

Here's how three real students turned their self-awareness into action:

Story 1: Arjun – From Gamer to Game Developer

Arjun loved playing video games. Everyone told him it was a waste of time—until he joined a coding club. Now, he's learning Python and dreams of designing games that tell Indian stories.

Story 2: Farah – From Helping to Healing

Farah loved helping her friends sort out their problems. A teacher told her about careers in psychology. Today, Farah wants to become a child counselor.

Story 3: Devika – The Maths Magician

Devika scored well in math and loved solving puzzles. She didn't want to become an engineer, but her career counselor introduced her to data science. Now she's exploring analytics and machine learning.

Try It Yourself
Here's a quick self-exploration activity.

My Career Mirror

Step 1: List 3 things you love doing.
Example: Acting, solving math problems, caring for animals

Step 2: List 3 subjects you enjoy most.
Example: English, Biology, Computer Science

Step 3: List 3 skills you're proud of.
Example: Speaking clearly, writing creatively, helping friends

Step 4: Think of a career that matches these.
Example: Veterinarian, science communicator, digital artist

Think & Reflect

1. What's more important to you: doing a job that pays a lot, or one that gives you happiness? Why?
2. If money and marks didn't matter, what would you do every day?
3. Do you feel pressure to choose a certain career because of parents, friends, or society?

Pause and write down your answers in a journal. Reflecting helps you make choices based on YOU.

Let's Revise (Mind Map Summary)

plaintext

CopyEdit

```
            KNOW YOURSELF
                |
  -------------------------------------
  |             |               |
Interests     Skills          Personality & Values
(What you     (What you're     (How you like to work,
 enjoy)       good at)          what matters to you)
```

Helps build your ideal career fit

Reduces confusion about what to study

Makes decisions more meaningful

Check Yourself

MCQs

1. Which of these is a soft skill?

A. Coding

B. Painting
C. Communication
D. Calculating Speed
Answer: C

2. Self-awareness helps students to:
A. Copy others
B. Choose random subjects
C. Select careers aligned with their strengths
D. Avoid learning anything new
Answer: C

Short Answer
1. What is the difference between interest and skill?
2. Name two skills that are important for teamwork.

Case-Based Question

Aman loves storytelling, performs well in English, and enjoys social issues. What career options could suit him? Justify your answer based on interests and skills.

Explore a Future in Careers

Self-awareness can lead you to diverse careers:

If You Like...	You Might Enjoy Careers Like...
Problem-solving	Engineer, Data Analyst, Architect
Storytelling	Journalist, Screenwriter, Lawyer
Helping Others	Social Worker, Nurse, Teacher

Organizing	Event Planner, Project Manager
Creativity	Animator, UX Designer, Content Creator

Pro Tip: *No interest is "too small." Every strength can become a superpower in the right career.*

Beyond the Book: Research Activity

Project Idea: "Interview Your Future Self"
Create a fictional interview with your 25-year-old self. Use these prompts:

- What career do you do now?
- What subjects helped you get there?
- What advice would you give your younger self?

You can write it, record it, or present it in class. Share what you learned from imagining your future.

Final Thought

Knowing yourself is the first and most important step in career planning. Before you chase any job title, college course, or exam score—take time to explore who you are. That one step can change your whole future.

"Don't ask children what they want to be. Ask them what problems they want to solve."
— Jaime Casap

Chapter 2

Explore the World of Work

Career Clusters and Options

Imagine walking into a massive Career Mela (career fair). There are stalls everywhere — one has robots coding away, another plays classical music, yet another is full of people wearing lab coats, running experiments. There's someone drawing storyboards for a movie, and someone else running a campaign to save the environment.

Welcome to the world of careers — vibrant, diverse, and full of possibilities!

Many students think of only 5–6 popular jobs: doctor, engineer, teacher, IAS officer, pilot, or cricketer. But the truth is, the world is filled with thousands of unique professions — and many are yet to be invented!
This chapter will help you discover career clusters, understand how

they work, and explore which ones match your personality and interests.

Explore the Concept: What are Career Clusters?

Career clusters are groups of jobs and industries that are related by knowledge, skills, or work environment.

Think of clusters like "neighborhoods" in a city. Each has its own kind of people, culture, and activities. You may feel more at home in some neighborhoods than others.

India's education and career system increasingly uses this concept to help students explore opportunities beyond traditional boundaries.

There are 6 Core Career Clusters

Cluster	Examples
1. STEM (Science, Technology, Engineering, Math)	Engineer, Data Analyst, Biotech Researcher
2. Commerce & Business	Chartered Accountant, Entrepreneur, Stockbroker
3. Arts & Creative Media	Filmmaker, Designer, Animator, Photographer
4. Social Sciences & Humanities	Lawyer, Historian, Psychologist, IAS Officer
5. Education & Health	Teacher, Counselor, Doctor, Therapist
6. Skilled Trades & Vocational Fields	Electrician, Chef, Mechanic, Fashion Tailor

In the Real World

Let's meet three students from different clusters.

Cluster: STEM

Ravi always loved math and machines. After interning at a drone startup, he decided to become a robotics engineer. Now he's working on AI-powered farming bots that help Indian farmers.

Cluster: Arts & Creative

Amrita used to doodle everywhere. Her teacher introduced her to graphic design. She now creates logos and digital posters for brands on social media — and earns pocket money too!

Cluster: Education & Health

Jayshree loved biology and helping others. She explored nursing, physiotherapy, and nutrition. Eventually, she found her passion in becoming a child psychologist.

Try It Yourself: What's Your Cluster?

ACTIVITY: Match Your Interests to Clusters
Instructions: Put a next to all that apply to you.

STEM

• I enjoy solving logical puzzles.
• I'm curious about how things work.
• I like math, science, or tech.

Commerce & Business

- I like numbers and analyzing data.
- I enjoy planning events or making deals.
- I'm interested in finance, economics, or starting a business.

Arts & Media

- I express myself through music, art, or drama.
- I love storytelling and visuals.
- I enjoy designing, drawing, or creating content.

Humanities & Social Sciences

- I care about society, justice, and governance.
- I enjoy reading, writing, and debating.
- I'm interested in history, law, or philosophy.

Health & Education

- I like helping people grow or recover.
- I'm good at explaining ideas.
- I'm interested in medicine, fitness, or teaching.

Trades & Vocational

- I enjoy hands-on work or crafting.
- I like to fix, build, or cook things.
- I want to learn a skill that earns quickly.

Count your marks. Which cluster had the most? That might be where your strengths and interests lie!

Think & Reflect

1. Which cluster do you feel most connected to? Why?
2. Do your current subject choices support that cluster?
3. Which career cluster do your parents expect you to join? Is it the same as your preference?

TIP: Your career doesn't have to fit in only one cluster. Some careers are hybrids — like a social media data analyst (STEM + Media + Business).

Let's Revise – Visual Recap

plaintext
CopyEdit

Career Clusters	Groups of Related Jobs
STEM	Tech, Engineering, Science
Commerce	Business Finance, Management, Sales
Humanities	Law, Politics, Research
Education/Health	Teacher, Doctor, Counselor
Trades/Vocational	Mechanic, Chef, Technician

Helps you explore your strengths + discover career options!

Check Yourself

Multiple Choice

1. Which of the following careers is part of the Arts & Creative cluster?

A. Pharmacist

B. Data Scientist

C. Illustrator

D. Chartered Accountant

Answer: C

2. Which statement is false?

A. Career clusters help group jobs with similar skills

B. STEM only includes engineering

C. A person can fit in more than one cluster

D. Career clusters include creative and vocational careers

Answer: B

Short Answer

1. Name any two career clusters and one profession under each.
2. How can exploring career clusters help you make better subject choices?

Case-Based Reasoning

Shreya loves sketching, writing poetry, and organizing school campaigns. Which clusters might suit her, and why?

Explore a Future in Career Planning

Here are some cool emerging roles from each cluster:

Cluster	Emerging Careers
STEM	AI Engineer, Climate Scientist, Drone Technician
Business	Digital Marketer, Blockchain Analyst, Startup Founder
Arts	Game Designer, Content Creator, UI/UX Designer
Humanities	Policy Analyst, Human Rights Lawyer, Sociologist
Health & Ed	Sports Psychologist, Speech Therapist, EdTech Trainer
Vocational	Solar Panel Technician, Organic Chef, App-based Mechanic

India's job market is evolving fast. Careers in green energy, mental health, data science, gaming, and social impact are booming.

Beyond the Book: Research Activity

Project Idea: "Create Your Career Cluster Poster"

Pick one career cluster. Design a colorful chart/poster including:

- Cluster name
- 5–7 jobs
- Skills needed
- Education/training required
- Any Indian success story or example

You can submit it as a physical poster or a digital slide.

Final Thought

Exploring career clusters gives you direction without pressure. It helps you narrow down your interests without choosing a final job yet. Think of it as creating your career GPS — once you know the zone, you can zoom in!

"Not all those who wander are lost — but those who explore often find the best paths."

Chapter 3

Career Paths in India and Beyond

Imagine this:

• Ishaan from Lucknow builds a startup that helps farmers use AI-powered irrigation.

• Fatima, raised in a small town in Kerala, becomes a legal advisor at the United Nations.

• Aarav, who once loved building models from LEGO, now designs eco-friendly homes in Germany.

What do they have in common?

They each found their career path—some right here in India, and some globally. Today, careers are not limited by geography. Whether you want to become a chef in Paris, a YouTuber from your village, or a tech expert working for ISRO, the world is open—if you plan well.

This chapter helps you explore the types of career paths available within India and internationally, how to approach them, and how to choose a path that aligns with your life goals.

Explore the Concept: What Is a Career Path?

A career path is the journey from student life to professional life—shaped by your:

- Subject choices
- Education and training
- Personal goals and circumstances
- Location (urban/rural, India/global)
- Passion and perseverance

It's not a straight line. You may shift directions or combine multiple paths. For example:

- An artist becomes an art therapist
- A teacher becomes a curriculum designer
- A coder starts their own ed-tech startup

In the Real World: Career Pathways in India

India's fast-growing economy offers career opportunities across sectors:

1. Government Careers (Sarkari Jobs)

- UPSC, State PSCs, SSC, Railways, Defense (NDA/AF)
- **Careers:** IAS/IPS/IFS, forest officers, customs, income tax officers, clerks
- Exam-based, requires dedication and strategy

2. STEM & Technology

- Software engineers, data scientists, AI/ML experts, cybersecurity professionals

• **Key recruiters:** TCS, Infosys, Wipro, ISRO, DRDO, Indian startups

• **Courses:** B.Tech, BCA, Data Science certifications

3. Healthcare & Medicine

• Doctors, pharmacists, radiologists, paramedics, psychologists

• Entry via NEET, paramedical courses, B.Sc. Nursing, or AYUSH

4. Creative & Performing Arts

• Artists, actors, musicians, filmmakers, designers

• **Schools:** NID, FTII, Srishti, NSD

• Freelancing and entrepreneurship also common

5. Business & Management

• MBA, entrepreneurship, finance, marketing, human resources

• Institutes: IIMs, DU, NMIMS, Symbiosis, Start-up India programs

6. Education & Social Work

• Teachers, researchers, NGO professionals, civil society leaders

• B.Ed., M.A., MSW (Social Work), or fellowships like Teach For India

7. Skilled & Vocational Trades

• Electricians, chefs, technicians, makeup artists, tailors

• ITIs, NSDC training centres, PMKVY programs

India's National Education Policy (NEP 2020) promotes equal value for academic and vocational paths.

Career Paths Beyond Borders

Students from India are increasingly exploring global careers. Here's how:

1. Studying Abroad

- **Popular countries:** USA, UK, Canada, Germany, Australia, Japan
- **Exams:** SAT, IELTS, TOEFL, GRE
- **Fields:** Tech, management, design, law, medicine, sustainability

2. Working Abroad After Study

- Post-study work visas (e.g., Canada's PGWP, UK's Graduate Route)
- Demand for Indian STEM graduates, nurses, researchers

3. Remote Global Work

- Freelancers, consultants, coders working with global clients via Upwork, Fiverr, GitHub
- **Fields:** UI/UX, content writing, AI, web development

4. Global NGOs and Policy Careers

- UN, Amnesty, WWF, WHO, Gates Foundation
- Requires social sciences, law, public health or international relations background

Try It Yourself: Identify Your Target Zone

ACTIVITY: Where Would You Like to Work?

Put a check mark next to all that apply:

- I'd love to serve India through government service
- I want to work for a startup or MNC in India

- I'm interested in freelancing from anywhere
- I'd love to study or work abroad
- I want to work on social or environmental issues
- I want a career that blends global & local impact

Now write a short paragraph:
"My ideal career would be… because…"
This exercise helps you define your zone of interest and intention.

Think & Reflect

1. Do you want to stay in India for your career? Why or why not?
2. Which Indian city or global country excites you as a place to work?
3. Do your current subject choices align with this path?

Tip: There's no "best" place to work—it depends on what you want from life: security, money, freedom, impact, or travel.

Let's Revise – Visual Snapshot

plaintext
CopyEdit
CAREER PATHWAYS

IN INDIA
Govt Jobs STEM & Tech
Healthcare Arts & Media
Business Education & NGO
Skilled Trades
BEYOND INDIA
Study Abroad Work Visas
Remote Freelance Global NGOs

Each path needs planning: subjects + skills + opportunities

Check Yourself

Multiple Choice

1. What is NOT a vocational career?
A. Tailor
B. Electrician
C. Surgeon
D. Plumber
Answer: C

2. Which of these careers may require international exams like GRE or IELTS?
A. UPSC
B. B.Ed.
C. Studying in Canada
D. PMKVY certification
Answer: C

Short Answer

1. Name three government career options and their required qualifications.
2. What are the benefits and challenges of working abroad?

Case-Based Reasoning

Aditi is passionate about sustainability and wants to work in international climate policy. Which study path and skills should she focus on to achieve this?

Explore a Future in Global & Indian Careers

Dream	Real Career Option
Serve your nation	IAS, Armed Forces, Agri-Tech Innovator
Travel the world	Airline Pilot, Travel Writer, UN Consultant
Earn well	FinTech, Data Science, Cybersecurity
Help people	Psychologist, Teacher, Rural Development Officer
Be creative	Filmmaker, Game Designer, Music Composer

Today's careers are fluid—you can work in India for a global company, or live abroad and work for an Indian startup!

Beyond the Book: Research Activity

Project: Map a Career Path

Choose a career you're interested in. Create a timeline or flowchart with:

- High school subjects required
- Higher education degrees/courses
- Any national/international exams needed
- Skills to develop
- Possible job roles at age 25

Present your "Career Map" in a visual format (poster, digital slide, etc.)

Final Thought

Your career path is yours to create. You may take small steps, take detours, or switch lanes—and that's okay.
What matters is having a map, a sense of direction, and the willingness to learn.

"The world is full of paths. You don't have to follow someone else's. You can create your own."

Chapter 4

Aligning Subjects with Career Goals

When Priya chose History and Political Science in Grade 11, people asked, "You're not taking Science? Are you sure?"
When Arnav picked Physics, Chemistry, and Maths, everyone assumed he was going to become an engineer. But he wanted to become an astrophysicist. These stories are common. Why? Because in India, students often choose subjects based on trends, peer pressure, or family advice—not based on their career goals. But here's the truth: your subject choices from Grade 9 onwards can open or close doors to your dream career. That's why this chapter will guide you in matching your subjects to your strengths, interests, and career aspirations.

Explore the Concept: Why Subject Choices Matter

Your subjects are your tools. The better you choose them, the better prepared you'll be for:

- College entrance exams (JEE, NEET, CUET, SAT, etc.)

- Competitive exams (UPSC, SSC, CLAT, etc.)
- Vocational training or apprenticeships
- Real-world career tasks (writing, coding, marketing, managing)

So how do you align your subjects with your goals? By understanding:

1. Your interests and skills (Chapter 1)
2. Your target career path (Chapter 3)
3. The academic qualifications needed

Subject Streams in India (Grades 11–12)

Science Stream

Key Subjects	Career Paths
Physics, Chemistry, Maths (PCM)	Engineering, Architecture, Defence, Data Science
Physics, Chemistry, Biology (PCB)	Medicine, Nursing, Biotech, Pharmacy
PCMB (All four)	Medicine + Engineering options, Research, Astrobiology
Optional: Computer Science, Physical Education, Psychology	Adds skill variety, supports tech/ health careers

Commerce Stream

Key Subjects	Career Paths
Accountancy, Business Studies, Economics	CA, MBA, Banking, Entrepreneurship
Maths (Optional)	Required for B.Com (Hons), Economics, Actuarial Science

Optional: Informatics Practices, Marketing, Legal Studies	Supports digital business, law, analytics careers

Arts/Humanities Stream

Key Subjects	Career Paths
History, Political Science, Geography, Sociology	Law, Journalism, Civil Services, Education, NGO work
Psychology, Philosophy, Fine Arts, Language subjects	Careers in mental health, design, content writing, linguistics
Optional: Economics, Maths	Opens doors to social sciences, economics, analytics

In the Real World: Subject-Career Matches

Want to be a Doctor?

- **Subjects:** Biology, Chemistry, Physics (PCB)
- **Entrance:** NEET
- **Backup options:** Psychology, Nursing, Paramedical Sciences

Want to be an Architect?

- **Subjects:** PCM (with Mathematics mandatory)
- **Entrance:** NATA, JEE B.Arch
- **Skills:** Drawing, creativity, logical reasoning

Want to be a Lawyer?

- **Subjects:** Any stream, but Political Science, English, History help
- **Entrance:** CLAT, LSAT
- **Bonus:** Good reading & analytical thinking skills

Want to be a CA or Finance Professional?

- **Subjects:** Accountancy, Business Studies, Economics
- **Entrance:** CA Foundation, CUET (B.Com)
- Math is optional but helpful

Want to be in Media or Content Creation?

- **Subjects:** English, Psychology, Sociology, Fine Arts
- **Courses:** Mass Comm, BMM, Film Studies
- **Bonus:** Portfolio, YouTube/blog, storytelling skills

Try It Yourself: Subject-Career Alignment Map

ACTIVITY: Match Your Goals to Subjects

Step 1: Write your top 2–3 career interests
Example: Psychologist, Lawyer, Filmmaker

Step 2: Research what subjects are most helpful for each
Example:

- Psychologist → Biology, Psychology, Sociology
- Lawyer → History, Political Science, English
- Filmmaker → Fine Arts, Literature, Mass Media Studies

Step 3: Create a table like this:

Career Goal Required/ Helpful Subjects	My Current Subjects
Psychologist Psychology, Biology	✓Psychology, X Biology

Now reflect: Do your subjects support your goals? If not, what changes can you make?

Think & Reflect

1. What subjects do you currently study?
2. Do they align with the career you're aiming for?
3. Have you chosen any subject just because someone else told you to?

Tip: It's okay to switch goals. But choosing the right subjects gives you more flexibility, not less.

Let's Revise – Summary Snapshot

plaintext
CopyEdit

SUBJECT-CAREER ALIGNMENT

STREAM	CAREERS
Science	Doctor, Engineer, Researcher
Commerce	CA, MBA, Banker, Entrepreneur
Humanities	Lawyer, UPSC, Journalist, Psychologist
Vocational	Chef, Mechanic, Fashion Designer, Technician

- Know your goal
- Choose supporting subjects
- Stay open to flexibility

Check Yourself

Multiple Choice

1. Which subject is essential for becoming a Chartered Accountant (CA)?

A. Political Science
B. Accountancy
C. Biology
D. Physics
Answer: B

2. If you want to study psychology in college, which subject is helpful in school?
A. Business Studies
B. Geography
C. Psychology
D. Chemistry
Answer: C

Short Answer

1. Name one career each from Science, Commerce, and Humanities.
2. What subject combinations would help you prepare for both NEET and AI/ML careers?

Case-Based Reasoning

Rohan loves biology and coding. He wants a career in healthcare and technology. Suggest a subject combination and future options.

Explore a Future in Hybrid Careers

The world now needs multidisciplinary thinkers. Check out these hybrid career paths:

Career	Suggested Subjects
Bioinformatics	Biology + Computer Science
Legal Tech	Political Science + Computer Science
Science Communication	Physics + English
Sports Psychology	Physical Education + Psychology
Fashion Business	Fashion Studies + Business Studies

NEP 2020 supports combining arts, science, and commerce. Many schools now allow cross-stream subject selection.

Beyond the Book: Research Activity

Project: My Subject-Career Planner

Create a 1-page planner that includes:

- Your dream careers (2–3 options)
- Matching subjects
- Colleges or exams needed
- Skill-building ideas
- Backup career choices

Present it in class or keep it for your portfolio!

Final Thought

The right subject choices are not about impressing others—they're about preparing yourself. Whether you choose PCB, PCM, Humanities, or a mix of all—do it consciously. Your subject is your stepping stone. Let it lead you where your heart wants to go.

"Choose a subject that excites your mind—because you'll be working with it for years to come."

Chapter 5

Skills that Matter

Academic & Life Skills for Career Success

Imagine two students preparing for the same job interview.
• One has top marks but struggles to speak confidently.
• The other knows how to collaborate, think critically, and explain ideas clearly.

Who gets hired?

In today's world, marks alone aren't enough. Employers and colleges look for skills — the abilities that help you think, adapt, solve problems, and work with people.

This chapter will help you understand the two kinds of skills that shape careers:

1. Academic Skills – What you learn through subjects and study
2. Life Skills (21st-Century Skills) – The skills that prepare you for

the real world
Let's dive into why these skills matter—and how you can build them.

Explore the Concept: What Are Career-Ready Skills?

Career-ready skills are a mix of knowledge, abilities, and attitudes that make you effective in school, college, jobs, and life.

Type of Skill	Examples
Academic	Reading, Writing, Numeracy, Research
Life / Core	Communication, Teamwork, Time Management
Higher-Order	Critical Thinking, Creativity, Leadership
Digital	Typing, Using Excel, Coding, Online Research

The NEP 2020 promotes skill-based education to prepare students for real-life challenges, not just exams.

Academic Skills: More Than Just Marks

Academic skills are the foundation of learning. But they go beyond rote learning or test scores.

Key Academic Skills for Career Success

Skill	Why It Matters
Reading Comprehension	Helps you understand instructions, emails, reports
Writing Skills	Useful for essays, resumes, communication

Numeracy	Needed in finance, research, science, everyday budgeting
Research	Crucial for college projects, career exploration, problem-solving
Note-Taking & Organizing Info	Helps in exams, interviews, workplace training

Example: A marketing career may not require physics, but it will need strong writing, research, and presentation skills.

Life Skills: The Real Game-Changers

Life skills are what help you function, thrive, and lead in any situation.

10 Essential Life Skills for the 21st Century

1. Communication – Speak and write clearly
2. Collaboration – Work in teams, respect differences
3. Critical Thinking – Analyze and solve problems logically
4. Creativity – Think outside the box, generate new ideas
5. Adaptability – Stay flexible in changing situations
6. Leadership – Motivate, manage, and support others
7. Time Management – Prioritize tasks and meet deadlines
8. Digital Literacy – Use technology confidently and responsibly
9. Emotional Intelligence – Understand and manage emotions
10. Self-Motivation – Stay driven without needing reminders

No matter your career*—doctor, designer, or data analyst—these skills make you a better professional and person.*

In the Real World: Why Skills Matter

Case 1: Komal – The Confident Coder

Komal wasn't the top student, but she built websites and participated in coding hackathons. Her communication and problem-solving skills helped her land an internship at a tech startup—before she even finished school!

Case 2: Tanish – The Thoughtful Teacher

Tanish always loved history, but he also volunteered as a peer mentor. His empathy and leadership led him to pursue a career in teaching—and he's now studying educational psychology.

Try It Yourself: Rate Your Skills

ACTIVITY: Self-Assessment Tracker

Rate yourself from 1 (beginner) to 5 (excellent)

Skill	My Rating (1–5)
Writing clearly	✓
Working in groups	✓
Solving problems	✓
Managing my time	✓
Using Google tools	✓
Coming up with new ideas	✓

Now answer:

- Which 2 skills are your strongest?
- Which 2 skills need improvement?
- How can you work on them this month?

Think & Reflect

1. Do you feel confident speaking in front of a group? Why or why not?
2. How do you usually respond to problems: avoid them, panic, or solve them?
3. What's one life skill you admire in others and want to build in yourself?

Tip: Skills grow with effort. You don't have to be perfect—you just have to be consistent.

Let's Revise – Mind Map Summary

plaintext
CopyEdit

CAREER SUCCESS =	ACADEMIC + LIFE SKILLS
Academic Skills	Life Skills
• Reading	• Communication
• Writing	• Teamwork
• Maths/Numeracy	• Problem-Solving
• Research	• Creativity
• Organizing Info	• Time Management
• Emotional Intelligence	• Adaptability & Leadership

Digital Skills = Must-have for all modern careers

Check Yourself

Multiple Choice

1. Which of the following is a life skill?
A. Algebra
B. Problem-Solving
C. Reading a textbook
D. Memorizing dates
Answer: B

2. What skill helps you express your thoughts clearly?
A. Drawing
B. Critical Thinking
C. Communication
D. Budgeting
Answer: C

Short Answer

1. Name two academic skills and how they are used in the workplace.
2. Why is emotional intelligence important in careers like teaching or nursing?

Case-Based Reasoning

Aditya is brilliant in science but often misses deadlines and struggles in group work. What skills should he focus on, and how might this impact his future career?

Explore a Future Built on Skills

Career-ready professionals are those who combine their knowledge with practical abilities.

Career	Key Skills
Software Developer	Coding, Problem-Solving, Teamwork
Lawyer	Research, Communication, Argumentation
Designer	Creativity, Visual Thinking, Client Management
Teacher	Patience, Emotional Intelligence, Speaking Skills
Entrepreneur	Decision-Making, Risk-Taking, Adaptability

Most skills are transferable—once you build them, they help you across subjects and jobs.

Beyond the Book: Skill-Building Activity

Project: "My Skill Challenge"
Choose one skill you want to build this month (e.g., time management).

Plan:

- What will you do daily/weekly?
- How will you track progress?
- How will you reflect at the end?

Document your journey with photos, journals, or voice notes. Share with a friend or teacher.

Final Thought

Marks may get you into college, but skills will carry you through life. Build them now, brick by brick, and you'll walk into any room—interview, classroom, or boardroom—with confidence.

"Skill is the currency of the 21st century. Start earning it now."

Chapter 6

The Role of Internships, Volunteering, and Projects

Imagine two students applying for the same college course in journalism.

• One has excellent marks.

• **The other has decent marks plus:**

A blog with 20 published articles

A short internship with a local newspaper

A volunteering certificate from a media literacy NGO

Who do you think stands out?

Real-world experience is becoming just as important as academic scores.

That's where internships, volunteering, and projects come in.

This chapter will teach you how these activities:

• Help you test your interests

- Build your resume and confidence
- Connect you with real professionals
- Strengthen college applications and career direction

Let's see how to learn by doing.

Explore the Concept: What Are Internships, Volunteering, and Projects?

Term	What It Means	Example
Internship	Short-term, practical work experience, usually at an organization	A 4-week internship at a graphic design firm
Volunteering	Helping a cause, NGO, or community project without pay	Teaching kids at a weekend learning center
Student Projects	Self-driven or guided activities to apply your skills	Creating a YouTube channel or science model

They help you understand what working in the real world feels like — the schedules, expectations, creativity, and teamwork involved.

In the Real World: Student Stories

Case 1: Aarav's Internship in Agriculture

Aarav wanted to study agricultural science. His school arranged a 3-week internship on a farm using drone irrigation. He learned hands-on skills and later used this experience in his college essay.

Case 2: Zara's Volunteering in Rural Health

Zara volunteered with a health NGO during summer break. She helped spread awareness about menstrual hygiene in villages. That sparked her passion to study public health.

Case 3: Kavya's Student-Led Project

Kavya loved storytelling. She created a digital comic series on mental health and uploaded it on Instagram. Now she's applying to design schools with her portfolio.

Try It Yourself: Find Your First Opportunity

Here's how to get started—even as a school student:

- Look for student-friendly platforms like Internshala, Younity, The Climber, Talerang
- Ask your school counselor about school partnerships
- Approach local businesses, startups, or professionals politely with a resume

For Volunteering:

- Join local NGOs (e.g., Goonj, Robin Hood Army, Teach For India)
- Volunteer at school events, campaigns, or library drives
- Use UN Volunteers India or iVolunteer

For Projects:

- Start a podcast, blog, YouTube channel, or Instagram series
- Build a science model or mobile app
- **Participate in competitions:** ATL Marathon, Google Code to Learn, Science Fairs

Think & Reflect

1. What area do you want to explore through an internship or project?
2. What social cause are you passionate about for volunteering?
3. What is one personal project you could start this month?

Tip: Don't wait for the "perfect" opportunity. Start small, stay consistent, and grow big.

Let's Revise – Summary Snapshot

plaintext
CopyEdit

Practical Experience Pathways

Activity	What It Builds
Internship	Real-world skills, exposure
Volunteering	Social responsibility, teamwork
Projects	Creativity, initiative, portfolio

Adds to resume, college forms, personal growth

Check Yourself

Multiple Choice

1. Which of the following is not an example of volunteering?
A. Teaching children for free
B. Helping in a blood donation drive
C. Attending a coaching class
D. Planting trees with a local NGO

Answer: C

2. What is the main benefit of student-led projects?

A. Memorization

B. Passive learning

C. Hands-on experience

D. Time-pass

Answer: C

Short Answer

1. Name two platforms where students can find internships.
2. How does volunteering help in career planning?

Case-Based Reasoning

Samar is interested in environmental science. Suggest one internship, one volunteer activity, and one student project he can do before Grade 12 to strengthen his college application.

Explore a Future through Early Experience

Here are examples of experience-rich career starters:

Career Interest	Possible Early Experience
Journalism	Start a school newsletter or blog
Medicine	Volunteer at health camps or shadow a doctor
Law	Attend mock trials or write on legal topics
Engineering	Build simple machines or join a robotics club

Psychology	Help with peer mentoring or write mental health articles
Business	Run a school store or organize a fundraiser

Experience not only teaches—it also signals your seriousness to future colleges and employers.

Beyond the Book: Action Plan

Project: Plan a 30-Day Mini-Experience

1. Pick a topic or field (e.g., storytelling, teaching, science, cooking)
2. Set a goal (e.g., publish 4 blog posts, teach 5 kids, create 1 short film)
3. Plan weekly steps
4. Keep a reflection journal or video log
5. Share your project with classmates or teachers

Use this format to create a basic experience portfolio for college or job interviews.

Final Thought

Internships, volunteering, and projects show that you're more than your grades. They reflect your curiosity, commitment, and initiative. These real-world experiences are like windows — they let you peek into your future career.

"You don't need to wait to grow up to get experience. Start learning by doing—right now."

Chapter 7

Decision-Making and Goal Setting

Your Career Compass

You're at a crossroads.

Do you take commerce or science? Apply for engineering or design school? Choose an internship with a startup or a local NGO?

At this point, your decisions start shaping your future. But how do you make the right ones?

Meet Riya, a Grade 10 student who loves both psychology and business. She's unsure which career to pursue. But once she learns how to set SMART goals, her confusion turns into clarity.

In this chapter, you'll discover:

- How to make informed decisions about your future
- The SMART way to set goals

• Tools and tips to build decision-making confidence
Let's begin your journey from confusion to clarity.

Explore the Concept: What Is Career Decision-Making?

Career decision-making means choosing what to pursue and why — based on your self-awareness, opportunities, and goals.

It's a Process, Not a One-Time Event:

1. Understand Yourself – Know your interests, skills, and values
2. Explore Options – Research fields, courses, careers
3. Evaluate Fit – Match your preferences with career realities
4. Set Goals – Choose the direction and build a plan
5. Take Action – Move step by step with feedback
6. Revise if Needed – Stay flexible

"You don't need to have it all figured out. You just need to take the next best step."

Decision-Making Techniques for Teens

Let's explore three common tools:

1. SWOT Analysis

Helps you evaluate your Strengths, Weaknesses, Opportunities, and Threats.

SWOT Element	Example
Strength	Good at coding, confident speaker
Weakness	Poor time management
Opportunity	Free summer bootcamp in AI
Threat	Financial constraints for private college

2. Decision Matrix

Compare options based on criteria like interest, salary, effort, and future growth.

Option	Interest	Effort	Growth Score (Out of 10)
Law 8	6	9	23
Design 9	7	7	23
Coding 7	5	10	22

Now you can make a data-backed decision.

3. 5-3-1 Rule

- List your top 5 career ideas
- Narrow it to 3 realistic ones based on research
- Choose 1 goal to focus on this year

SMART Goals: Your Career GPS

SMART is a powerful tool to convert vague dreams into actionable goals.

Letter	Meaning	Example
S	Specific	"I want to improve my Python coding skills"
M	Measurable	"By building 3 Python projects in 3 months"
A	Achievable	"Using free online tutorials and 4 hours/ week"
R	Relevant	"Because I want to apply for a data science internship"
T	Time-bound	"I will finish all projects by September 30"

Goal: "I will complete 3 Python projects using online courses within 3 months to prepare for a data science internship."

In the Real World: How Teens Use SMART Goals

Tanmay:

SMART Goal – Complete a YouTube video editing course in 4 weeks and build a demo reel.
Outcome – Landed a freelance video editing gig on Fiverr.

Ayesha:

SMART Goal – Score 90+ in Accountancy and Business Studies by doing 2 practice papers weekly for 3 months.
Outcome – Cracked her commerce stream target and improved focus.

Neeraj:

SMART Goal – Volunteer 20 hours with an animal shelter and blog about the experience.
Outcome – Found his passion in veterinary sciences.

Try It Yourself: Your First SMART Goal

Follow this template:
1. What do you want to achieve?
→ (e.g., improve communication skills)
2. Why is it important to you?
→ (e.g., to prepare for debate competitions)
3. How will you measure success?
→ (e.g., participate in 3 debates this term)
4. What's your timeline?
→ (e.g., 2 months)
Write your SMART goal in this format:

"I will [specific action] by [deadline] using [methods/resources] to achieve [purpose]."

Think & Reflect

1. What's one decision you made in the past year that shaped your career interest?
2. How do you currently make decisions — based on logic, emotions, or advice?
3. What's one habit you can build this month using SMART goal-setting?

Let's Revise – Visual Summary

plaintext
CopyEdit
DECISION-MAKING + GOAL SETTING = CAREER SUCCESS
Steps to Make Career Decisions:
Know Yourself → Explore Options → Evaluate Fit → Set SMART

Goals → Take Action → Adjust as Needed

SMART GOAL FRAME:

S = Specific

M = Measurable

A = Achievable

R = Relevant

T = Time-bound

Check Yourself

Multiple Choice

1. What does "T" in SMART goals stand for?

A. True

B. Time-bound

C. Training

D. Trial

Answer: B

2. Which tool is used to analyze your strengths and weaknesses?

A. GPS

B. SWOT

C. SMART

D. Pie Chart

Answer: B

Short Answer

1. Write one SMART goal for your academic progress.
2. What are the 5 steps in the career decision-making process?

Case-Based Question

Sonia wants to become a psychologist but also likes filmmaking. She's confused. Guide her using any two decision-making tools from this chapter.

Beyond the Book: Project Idea

Career Compass Journal

• Keep a weekly log of small career decisions (e.g., which subject to choose, which webinar to attend)
• Write why you chose what you did, how you felt, and what you learned
• After a month, review your decisions and patterns
Helps you build self-awareness and reflect on your career direction

Final Thought

Career planning isn't a one-time event—it's a lifetime habit. Learning to make decisions and set SMART goals early in life helps you lead with clarity, purpose, and confidence.

"Clarity comes from action, not overthinking. Start small. Aim big. Reflect often."

Chapter 8

The World of Work

Sectors, Skills, and Job Types

Close your eyes and picture a typical "job."
Did you imagine someone in an office typing on a laptop? Or maybe a doctor treating a patient? Or a YouTuber filming a new video?
Work is everywhere – in labs, studios, farms, hospitals, classrooms, factories, and even in virtual worlds. The world of work has changed dramatically in the 21st century. Today's teenagers will enter jobs that didn't even exist 10 years ago.

So, how do you understand and prepare for this wide world of work?

In this chapter, you'll learn:

- Different sectors of the economy
- Skills needed in each sector
- Examples of jobs – traditional and modern
- How to explore work environments before choosing a path

Explore the Concept: What Is the World of Work?

The world of work refers to the vast universe of occupations, industries, and ways people earn a living. It includes:

- Formal jobs (e.g., teacher, engineer)
- Informal work (e.g., shop helper, family business)
- Freelance or gig work (e.g., video editor, food delivery)
- Entrepreneurship (starting your own business)

The 3 Main Economic Sectors

Sector	What It Involves	Examples of Jobs
Primary	Using natural resources	Farmer, miner, fisherman, horticulturist
Secondary	Processing raw materials into products	Factory worker, engineer, craftsman
Tertiary	Providing services	Doctor, lawyer, banker, teacher

Today, we also have:

- Quaternary Sector: Knowledge-based work – research, IT, data science
- Quinary Sector: Decision-makers – CEOs, policymakers, education leaders

In the Real World: Work in Modern India

India's youth are entering a world where careers are dynamic and often hybrid (part online, part offline). Here are emerging fields:

1. Digital India & Tech Careers

- App developer
- Cybersecurity analyst
- AI researcher
- Digital marketing strategist
- Data analyst

"India Stack" and UPI have created new digital economy careers.

2. Green Careers

- Solar panel installer
- Urban farming expert
- Environmental engineer
- Sustainability consultant

3. Creative and Communication Careers

- Influencer strategist
- Podcast producer
- Graphic designer
- Scriptwriter for OTT shows

4. Health and Wellness

- Mental health counselor
- Fitness coach
- Nutritionist
- Telehealth specialist

5. Vocational and Skilled Trades

- Electrician
- Auto technician
- Beautician
- Chef

Many of these offer high income and quick training options.

Career Clusters and Skills

You can also understand work better through career clusters – groups of similar jobs.

Career Cluster	Example Roles	Key Skills
STEM	Engineer, coder, biologist	Logical thinking, math, analysis
Arts & Media	Filmmaker, animator, journalist	Creativity, storytelling, tech
Business & Finance	Accountant, marketer, HR manager	Decision-making, communication
Education	Teacher, trainer, education tech	Empathy, leadership, planning
Hospitality	Chef, hotel manager, travel agent	Teamwork, customer service
Law & Governance	Lawyer, civil servant, judge	Argumentation, ethics, reasoning
Agri-Tech	Agri-scientist, supply chain expert	Problem-solving, sustainability

Try It Yourself: Career Sorting Game

Here are 10 career roles. Sort them into sectors or clusters.

(You can write in your notebook or do this as a group activity.)

- Lawyer
- Yoga instructor

• Mechanical engineer
• Digital artist
• Farmer
• Nurse
• Entrepreneur
• AI developer
• Event planner
• Marine biologist

Now think:
• Which ones interest you most?
• What skills do they require?
• What kind of lifestyle might come with these careers?

Think & Reflect

1. Which sector(s) do you see yourself in – Primary, Secondary, Tertiary, Quaternary, or Quinary? Why?
2. What do you think are the advantages of non-traditional careers (like YouTuber or podcast host)?
3. If your dream job didn't exist yet, what kind of new career could you imagine creating?

Let's Revise – Mind Map

plaintext
CopyEdit

```
                        WORLD OF WORK
                              |
          ---------------------------------------------------
          |              |              |                  |
Primary Sector   Secondary Sector   Tertiary     Emerging Fields
(Nature-based)   (Manufacturing)   (Services)   (Digital, Green, Gig)
    |                  |                 |              |
Farmer            Engineer        Doctor, Teacher  App Dev, Podcasting
```

Career Clusters → STEM | Arts | Business | Health | Law | Tech | Education

Check Yourself

MCQs

1. The sector where natural resources are directly used is called:

A. Quinary

B. Secondary

C. Primary

D. Tertiary

Answer: C

2. A job like "data analyst" belongs to which career cluster?

A. Hospitality

B. STEM

C. Law

D. Arts

Answer: B

Short Answers

1. Define the quaternary sector with two examples.
2. Name three skills required for success in the creative industry.
3. What is the difference between formal and gig work?

Case-Based Question

Ritu is interested in both agriculture and technology. Her uncle is a farmer, and she enjoys coding. Suggest two career paths that combine both fields and explain why they might suit her.

Beyond the Book: Project Idea

Career in a Day – Shadow & Interview

- Choose a career field (like health, law, tech, or art)
- Find someone working in that area (family, neighbor, or school alumni)
- **Interview them about:**
    - o What skills they use
    - o Their workday
    - o Challenges and rewards
- Present your learnings as a poster, PPT, or blog post

This builds real-world awareness and communication skills.

Final Thought

The world of work is not limited to offices or 9-to-5 routines. It's broad, diverse, and constantly evolving. You don't have to "fit in" to a job — you can create your own space by exploring, learning, and staying curious.

"Don't just choose a job. Choose a mission."
"Don't follow trends. Create value."

Chapter 9

Creating Your Career Roadmap

From Dream to Reality

Imagine you're on a road trip. You have a destination in mind, a map in your hand, and a list of stops along the way. Now imagine your career as a similar journey—with the destination being your dream job, and the roadmap guiding you step by step.

But how do you start? What if you're unsure about your destination? What if the road has detours?

This chapter is about creating your career roadmap—a flexible, evolving plan that helps you turn your career dreams into reality.

Explore the Concept: What Is a Career Roadmap?

A career roadmap is a structured plan that outlines your career goals, interests, skills, and the steps you need to take to achieve them.

Components of a Career Roadmap:

1. Self-awareness – Know your strengths, interests, and values.
2. Career research – Explore options and match them to your personality.
3. Short- and long-term goals – Define what success looks like for you.
4. Education and skill-building – Plan your academic and non-academic growth.
5. Experience and exposure – Seek internships, projects, or volunteer work.
6. Review and adapt – Revisit and revise your plan as you grow.

A career roadmap is like Google Maps – you need a destination, route options, and willingness to reroute when needed!

In the Real World: Why Career Planning Matters

Here's what happens when you plan your career early:

With a Roadmap	Without a Roadmap
Clear goals and steps	Confusion and indecision
Better use of high school and college time	Missed opportunities
Alignment with future job market trends	Risk of entering irrelevant fields
Stronger resumes, college apps, confidence	Lack of direction or clarity

Try It Yourself: Build Your Career Map (Worksheet Style)

Step 1: Dream Big

What is your ideal job or career dream?

- ______________________________

Step 2: Know Yourself

Write 3 strengths and 3 interests

Strengths:

1. ______________________________
2. ______________________________
3. ______________________________

Interests:

1. ______________________________
2. ______________________________
3. ______________________________

Step 3: Explore & Match

Match your interests to 3 possible careers

Interest	**Career Possibilities**
e.g., storytelling	journalist, filmmaker, copywriter

Step 4: Research Education & Skills Needed

Pick one of the careers and find out:

- Which subjects are useful in school?
- Is a degree or diploma required?
- What skills do professionals in this field have?

Step 5: Set SMART Goals

(Specific, Measurable, Achievable, Relevant, Time-bound)

Type	Example Goal
Short-term	Learn basic Python in 2 months
Medium-term	Score 80%+ in Class 10 Science
Long-term	Become a software engineer by 2032

Think & Reflect

1. What excites you the most about your dream career?
2. What is one skill or subject you can improve on now to help you in the future?
3. How will you handle it if your goals change in 2–3 years?

Let's Revise – Flowchart

plaintext

CopyEdit

START

↓

1. Know Yourself → Strengths + Interests + Values

↓

2. Explore Careers → Research Roles + Education + Lifestyle

↓

3. Match & Set Goals → SMART Goal-Setting

↓

4. Build Skills → Online Courses, Internships, Projects

↓

5. Track Progress → Revisit & Adjust Your Plan

↓

6. Dream → Plan → Act → Reflect → Repeat

Check Yourself

MCQs

1. A SMART goal must be:
A. Simple, Modern, Accurate, Realistic, Tangible
B. Specific, Measurable, Achievable, Relevant, Time-bound
C. Strategic, Managed, Artistic, Responsive, Targeted
Answer: B

2. Which of these is not part of a good career roadmap?
A. Knowing your strengths
B. Following your friend's career blindly
C. Setting short- and long-term goals
Answer: B

Short Answer

1. What are the three steps involved in researching a career?
2. Why should your career plan be flexible?

Case-Based Question

Aryan is good at science and loves robotics. But he's also curious about film-making. His parents want him to pursue engineering, but he's unsure. How can Aryan create a career roadmap that respects his interests and explores both paths?

Explore a Future in Career Planning

Did you know there are full-time careers helping others with their roadmaps?

- Career Counselor

• Life Coach
• School Guidance Expert
• HR Career Development Officer

These professionals use tests, mentoring, and tools to guide students, job seekers, and professionals toward their goals.

Beyond the Book: Project Idea

Make Your Career Vision Board
Materials: chart paper, old magazines, markers, glue, internet printouts
Steps:
• **Divide into 4 sections:** My Dream, My Skills, My Goals, My Inspiration
• Paste or draw images, quotes, role models, career symbols
• Present your vision board in class or in a group
• Update it every year as your interests grow!

This builds visual planning, motivation, and self-reflection.

Final Thought

Your dream job is not just a fantasy—it's a project that you can design, build, and shape. The roadmap you create today may evolve, but it will always remind you of your direction.
"Don't wait for the future. Build it. Step by step."
"Dreams become plans. Plans become action. Action becomes success."

Chapter 10

The Career Planning Toolkit

Apps, Resources, and Mentors

magine you want to climb Mount Everest. Would you go without a map, a guide, or the right gear? Of course not!

Just like adventurers need tools and experts, students need the right career planning toolkit—apps, resources, and mentors that guide them toward smart, informed decisions.
In this chapter, we'll explore practical tools and support systems to help you plan, track, and achieve your career goals with confidence.

Explore the Concept: What Is a Career Toolkit?

A career toolkit is a set of resources—digital, physical, and human—that helps you:

- Discover your strengths and interests
- Explore suitable career options

• Plan your education and skills
• Track your progress
• Get expert guidance

Your career toolkit should be personalized, updated often, and used actively.

In the Real World: Useful Tools and Platforms

1. Self-Assessment Tools

These help you understand your personality, learning style, and interests.

Tool	Purpose	Platform
MBTI (Myers-Briggs)	Personality type assessment	16personalities.com
Holland Code Test	Matches interests to career types	Truity, CareerOneStop
India's National Guidance Portal (NCVET)	Interest inventory and skill assessment	www.ncs.gov.in

Tip: Try multiple tests and compare results to find consistent themes.

2. Career Exploration Platforms

These help you explore various professions, salaries, education paths, and job trends.

Platform	Features
Careers360	Indian college and course discovery, career quizzes
BLS K-12 (US)	Job profiles, growth trends, educational paths

MyNextMove.org	Interest profiler and job-matching
Shiksha.com	Indian career options, admission help, scholarships
NCS Portal (India)	National career services, guidance counselors, job data

3. Learning & Upskilling Platforms

Skill-building is essential for career readiness.

Platform	What You Can Learn
Coursera/edX	Free/paid courses from IITs, Harvard, etc.
SWAYAM	Government e-learning for school and college students
Khan Academy	Math, science, economics (great for school help)
Coding Ninjas / WhiteHat Jr / Tinkerhub	Coding and AI skills for students
Internshala Trainings	Practical job-ready skills (resume, Excel, etc.)

4. Career Planning Apps

App	Features
Mindler	Career assessment, counseling, college finder
Univariety	School-based guidance platform
CareerGuide	Psychometric tests, mentoring, planning
LinkedIn	Build a professional profile, connect with mentors
Notion/Trello	Career and study planners for your roadmap

Mentors: The Human Side of Career Planning

While apps are amazing, nothing beats real conversations with people who've walked the path before you.

Types of Mentors

1. Teachers – Your subject teachers know your strengths well.
2. Parents & Family – Can share practical advice or real-world exposure.
3. Alumni – School or college seniors who've taken a path you like.
4. Professionals – Reach out to people on LinkedIn or during career fairs.
5. Career Counselors – Trained experts who can guide you through assessments and options.

"One mentor can save you years of confusion."

Try It Yourself

Task 1: Create Your Digital Career Toolkit

Open a Google Doc or Notion page and make your personal toolkit:

1. **Section 1:** Self-Assessment Results (Paste screenshots or scores)
2. **Section 2:** 5 Careers I Like – With their requirements, pros, and cons
3. **Section 3:** Learning Plan – Courses I'll take in next 6 months
4. **Section 4:** My Questions – What I want to ask my mentor
5. **Section 5:** Contacts – Teachers, counselors, or professionals to connect with

Task 2: Interview a Mentor

Pick one person—parent, teacher, cousin, coach—anyone you admire.

Ask:

- What career did you choose and why?
- What challenges did you face?
- What do you wish you knew at my age?
- What advice do you have for me?

Write a short reflection based on your conversation.

Think & Reflect

1. Which career platform or app surprised you the most? Why?
2. Who is someone in your life that you could reach out to as a mentor?
3. How often should you review and update your toolkit?

Let's Revise – Mind Map Style

plaintext

CopyEdit

```
Career Toolkit
│
├── Digital Tools
│   ├── Self-assessment (MBTI, NCVET)
│   ├── Career exploration (BLS, NCS)
│   ├── Learning platforms (SWAYAM, Coursera)
│   └── Planning apps (Mindler, Notion)
│
├── Mentorship
│   ├── Teachers
│   ├── Family
│   ├── Alumni
│   └── Counselors
│
└── Actions
```

├── Build digital portfolio
├── Reach out to mentors
└── Create learning roadmap

Check Yourself

MCQs

1. Which of these platforms is Indian and government-run?

A. Coursera

B. BLS

C. SWAYAM

D. MyNextMove

Answer: C

2. Which tool helps you match your personality with careers?

A. Excel

B. LinkedIn

C. MBTI

D. Canva

Answer: C

Short Answer

1. Name two free learning platforms and what they offer.
2. Why is mentorship important in career planning?

Case-Based Question

Ishita is a student who loves biology and wants to explore health careers. She's unsure if she should be a doctor or a researcher. Her school has limited guidance services. How can she build her toolkit to make better decisions?

Explore a Future in Career Services

Passionate about helping others find their path? You could consider:

• Career Counselor
• Educational Consultant
• HR Career Advisor
• Psychometric Test Designer
• College Admissions Coach

India's National Career Service is growing fast—and needs skilled youth.

Beyond the Book: Project Idea

Career App Review Challenge

• Pick one career guidance or learning app (e.g., Mindler, Khan Academy).
• Explore all its features for 1 week.
• Rate its usefulness for Indian high school students.
• Present your review in class or write a blog on it.
• Suggest features it could add for better engagement.

Outcome: Improves tech literacy + decision-making + critical thinking.

Final Thought

In the age of smartphones and smart boards, let your career planning be smart too. Don't wait to figure it all out later—use the tools, mentors, and platforms available now to explore, experiment,

and evolve.
"The right tools don't make the journey shorter—but they make it smarter."
"Your career toolkit is your compass—keep it sharp and up to date."

Full Book Summary

This book is your step-by-step roadmap to discovering, exploring, and planning your career path. Across 10 detailed and interactive chapters, you learn not just what careers exist, but how to choose the right one for you.

Chapter-wise Highlights

1. Know Yourself – Understand your personality, strengths, values, and interests to begin career discovery.
2. Discover the World of Careers – Explore industries and professions in STEM, arts, commerce, humanities, and vocational fields.
3. Matching Subjects with Careers – Learn how subject choices in school impact future education and career paths.
4. Understanding the 21st Century Job Market – Get to know evolving job roles, automation, and global trends.
5. Career Planning Step-by-Step – A practical guide to setting SMART goals, timelines, and action plans.
6. Education Pathways Explained – Learn about degrees, diplomas, vocational education, apprenticeships, and beyond.
7. Building Skills for Success – Focus on communication, leadership, digital literacy, emotional intelligence, and more.
8. Internships, Volunteering, and Experience – Understand the

importance of real-world exposure during high school.
9. Facing Challenges and Staying Motivated – Tackle self-doubt, peer pressure, setbacks, and learn how to stay on track.
10. The Career Planning Toolkit – Use apps, online platforms, personality tests, and mentors to continuously grow and adapt.

Key Themes

- Career planning is personal, flexible, and evolving.
- You are encouraged to experiment, reflect, and revise your choices.
- With the right tools, support, and mindset—you can create a career path that's right for you, not just popular.

Glossary of Key Terms

Term	Definition
Career Planning	The process of identifying career goals and developing a plan to achieve them.
Self-Assessment	Activities that help you understand your strengths, interests, and values.
Interest Profiler	A tool that matches your interests to potential careers.
Aptitude	Your natural ability or talent in a particular area.
Vocational Education	Training programs focused on hands-on skills for specific jobs.
Career Cluster	A group of similar careers or industries (e.g., health sciences, IT, agriculture).
Apprenticeship	A program combining on-the-job training with classroom instruction.
Internship	A short-term work experience to gain exposure to a career field.

Mentor	An experienced advisor who helps guide your career decisions.
Job Market	The current state of available jobs, salaries, and demand in various sectors.
Transferable Skills	Skills that are useful in many careers (e.g., teamwork, communication).
Entrepreneurship	Starting and running your own business or enterprise.
Career Counsellor	A trained professional who helps individuals make educational and career choices.
Portfolio	A collection of your work and achievements that showcase your skills.
NEP 2020	National Education Policy (India), which focuses on holistic, flexible, and competency-based learning.
NCF 2023	National Curriculum Framework, outlining curriculum goals under NEP 2020.
Digital Literacy	The ability to use digital tools, platforms, and media effectively.
Capstone Project	A final project that integrates and applies your learning to a real-world challenge.
Career Toolkit	A set of tools (apps, resources, mentors) used to support career exploration and planning.
SWAYAM	Indian Government's free online platform for learning and skill-building.